The Lilies of Dawn

The Lilies of Dawn

Vanessa Fogg

AnnorlundaBooks

Front cover illustration and design by Likhain.

Editing services from Francesca Forrest.

Published in the United States by Annorlunda Books.

Queries: info@annorlundaenterprises.com

First Edition

ISBN-13: 978-1-944354-12-1

The air is cool in the predawn light. I'm alone on the lake, poling my boat through the fields of floating lilies. All around me they grow — their leaves large enough to hold a small child, their pink flower buds held above the water on slender stalks, shut tight against the dark and chill. Even now, a hint of their sweet scent escapes. Here near the center of the lake, one would never know that something is amiss. Here the lilies still thrive, still carpet the water with their dense mats of blossoms and leaves.

The island draws close; I'm almost there. The roof of the shrine is dark angles against a lightening sky. There's white on the horizon, and the first blush of dawn. I rest for just a moment, standing in the prow of the boat. The sun will rise soon. The lilies aren't ready, not yet. But in a few weeks they will be. On that day, the sun will rise and the lilies will open to the light. Slowly they'll unfurl petals of deepest pink, and their full, heady scent — richer than jasmine or roses — will open, too.

Dawn will glow on the water as well as in the sky: the fields of dawn-lilies will bloom.

And then the ravenous birds will come.

So many visitors have come to stare at our flock. Wise sages, hoping to divine the cranes' mystery. Priests and monks and wandering shamans, promising to drive them away. Charlatans and simple curiosity-seekers. The visitors have dwindled as the years wear on, but we still get a few each season. They rent rooms and pay for meals. They don't make up for the pilgrims who used to come. They can't even begin to make up for the lost lily harvest. Some pay their respects at the Dawn Mother's shrine, and some don't.

None have ever driven the cranes away, not even for a moment.

So I'm not inclined to be impressed by the latest visitor. I'm airing out the shrine, washing down the inner walls and scrubbing off the mold and grime of the past rainy season, when the scrape of a boat on rough pebbles catches my ear. I come out in time to see the stranger walking up the path.

He's not a monk or a priest; I see that at a glance. He doesn't wear the golden robes of the *ankha* or the white and blue robes of the Saadu orders. Nor does he wear the red sash of one of our local shamans, or the traditional amulet of a sage. He's dressed simply, like one of our own men, in a light shirt and trousers. His black hair is unshorn, falling loose down his neck. He's young, not much older than me. And distractingly handsome—I see that at a glance, as well.

His dark eyes meet mine. He stops several paces away and bows, his hands pressed together above the level of his heart.

"Lady Kai," he says. "My name is Kevak. I've come to ask for your help."

No, he's not from here, whatever his dress might be. His accent is of the cities, of the cultured and educated classes. His skin is the pale golden hue of one who's never labored in the fields, under the pitiless sun. I say nothing, taken aback.

"I'm a doctor," he says into my silence. "I've come to learn about the lilies here, about how you make them into medicines and use them in your healing."

I can't help a bitter smile, then. "You're almost too late, Master Kevak," I say. "It will be a small harvest this year, as it has been for seasons. I can't say how much we'll be able to gather, or how much

9

nectar wine or petal-tea we'll be able to make. There's scarcely any left from the last harvest."

"I know." His gaze holds mine, gentle and solemn. "That's why I've come."

I feel something drop in my belly as he says this. To hear it said aloud — that we're in such a desperate way, that he knows our supply of dawn-lilies is almost gone and may fail altogether … Has he come just to catalogue medicinal recipes that will soon be useless, to note them into a book for history and curiosity's sake?

"You're not here to help with the cranes, then," I say. My voice is flat.

Something shifts in his manner: I catch an irrepressible gleam in his eye, the shadow of a smile on his lips. Some quiet, private amusement. Almost a hint of triumph in those beautiful eyes, dark as night and tapered like lily petals.

"I've come to learn about the lilies," he says smoothly, evenly. "But what I learn might help with the cranes, too."

That night I tell my mother about the visitor. Ari the neighbor girl has kept watch during the day while I've readied the shrine; Mother's been bathed and her bedclothes changed. She slept badly the night before, but Ari said she rested well today. She's able to sip the tea I hold to her lips, and I think she might be able to follow what I say.

"He trained at one of the royal academies. A scholar and doctor, both," I say. "He said that he's always been impressed with the effects of lily wine and medicines. He wants to understand how they're made, to examine the living lilies themselves. He thinks ..." My voice trails off. It sounds so strange. "He thinks that if he could understand the lilies' essence, their *ka*, he could find another way to give it to the cranes. A way to give them what they need, in such manner that they don't need to destroy our lily fields."

But she's not listening. She's gone rigid, her jaw clenched, her eyes withdrawn and glassy. I wait it out beside her. I stroke her hand and murmur her name. When the spell of pain passes, she sighs and her face is gray and beaded with sweat.

I wipe her face with a wet cloth. "Just a few weeks more," I tell her. "The blooming is almost here."

"Suna," she says, calling me by my sister's name. "Have you started preparing the shrine?"

"It's 'Kai,' Mother. And yes."

"I know your name!" she snaps, a bit of her old temper flaring. "I just misspoke." She closes her eyes. "A coat of new paint ... Gold leaf for offerings, do we have enough? Did you start weaving the palm garlands?"

"Yes."

"It's a special blooming, you know. The year-cycles of Fire and Crane have come together ... The shrine should look its best for the Dawn Mother."

"I know. The doctor brought offerings to us, coin and sheets of gold leaf. The shrine will look its best."

"Who?" She blinks at me, confused. "What doctor? Why is he here?" Her fingers pluck nervously at the bedcovers. "Suna, would you get me some water? There was something I wanted to tell you ..."

Her eyes have gone absent again, but at least this time she's not in pain. I give her a cup of pure water, scented with sweet-palm. Why does she call me "Suna," when it's me that she chose and Suna that she let go? She kept me here to serve the Dawn Mother even though I'm the younger one. She let my older sister live her own life.

I smooth back Mother's hair. It's gone dry and thin and gray. A year ago it was as thick and lustrous black as my own. Her skin has changed, too—paper-thin and soft. Dark bruises bloom on her arms and legs. The doctor, Kevak, had admitted that there was likely nothing he could do. He'd already heard the tale from others, of course: of the prickle-fever that swept our region last year, a bare month after the lily harvest. Mother used nearly all the lily wine on others, not leaving enough for herself. She had seemed to recover, but the prickle-fever is cunning. It seems to go away but hides in bones and nerves, coming out months later in a new, agonizing form. Kevak had seen it in his own patients. "I'm sorry," he'd said after listening to me describe Mother's illness. When the disease is this deeply rooted, there is only one cure.

Just a few weeks to the blooming, I think. We don't need much. A spoonful of fresh lily nectar, concentrated but taken before it ferments to wine.

"There was something I wanted to say," Mother says again, plaintive as a child. "It's a special blooming this year, remember …"

"I remember," I say.

She frowns, but then her eyes close again. I'd told Kevak to wait for the next day to pay his respects to her. Hopefully she'll have a clearer mind tomorrow. Hopefully she'll be able to greet him with dignity, as befits the Dawn Priestess. I'm not the one who should have met Kevak today. I'm not the one who should have accepted his offerings on behalf of the Dawn Mother. I'm not the one to be called "Lady." I'm not the one at all.

"Kai," she says, just as I think she's fallen asleep. "You said that someone from the capital has come to visit? Did he come here for the cranes?"

"Yes," I say.

I was twelve when I first saw the demon-cranes. I've seen them six times since, each year that they've come. But it's their first visit that I relive in my dreams.

It was the first day of the lily harvest. I remember the sun flashing over the lake, and the fierce color of the lilies unfurling. The pink dawn spreading, above and below. Mother stood at the front of our boat, her arms upraised, giving thanks to the Dawn Mother for her gift. All around us were the other villagers, waiting in their own boats. Pilgrims and visitors crowded the shore. Mother's voice fell into the perfect silence, each word like a clear stone dropped through still water. The light grew and grew. She lowered her arms, and there was a moment in which nothing moved. And then the cheers broke out, and I pushed off on my boat pole, eager to be off, and all around me everyone was doing the same.

I remember calling to my sister. She and her husband were in the next boat over. I remember laughing, making some foolish bet over who would collect the most nectar this year. It was the first year that Suna and I weren't in the same boat together, no longer a team. She was newly married, setting up her own household.

I was teasing Suna's husband, laughing at his mock-gruff responses. Excited voices rang out over the lake. The fleet of village boats slowly spread apart. I poled through the thick of the lilies, but Mother didn't direct me to any particular spot; her hands didn't reach out to the flowers. She was looking at the sky.

I looked up and saw them too.

Just a distant flock of birds. That's all it was. Black lines curving against the air, a graceful beat of movement. The lines of birds tightened together, broke apart, and tightened again. Then they were all together, and they were flying toward us, faster than any birds should fly, faster than anything should be.

They looked like cranes, but cranes of no size or marking that we'd ever seen. Pure white, except where their wing tips glowed with the fire of dawn. Dawn-pink their legs and feet and beaks. Even from a distance, you could see that color. Real cranes are loud; the high, whirring cries of a flock reach your ears before you ever see them. But these birds swept toward us from the east in utter silence.

They circled above the shrine in the middle of the lake. Fifty? More? They were beautiful— shining against the sky, a dream of grace and color. They landed like a cloud in the center of the lake. They began to feast.

"Hah!" my sister cried, breaking our shocked silence. Furiously, she began to pole toward the birds.

I followed, and others followed, all of us yelling and waving our arms. The birds ignored us as we neared. They bent their long, slender necks and plunged their bright bills into the hearts of the dawn-lilies.

Finally, the first boats drew to the edge of the flock. Finally, the birds scattered. They flew above us, so close that I felt the wind of their wing-beats on my face. They were huge, their wings as long as the length of a man. They churned the air; they were a storm of white lightning, of white sunlight and the living feathers of dawn. My hair whipped against my face; my breath caught. I saw those wing-tips glow, and I was blind with their brilliance.

And then the sky cleared, and the birds were scattered across the water. They were everywhere, standing near thickets of reeds, amidst the elephant grass at shore's edge, in the midst of the deepest water, bending to tear and suck at the lilies.

My sister was sobbing. "What are they?" she cried, and others echoed her. "What are they?" they pled of my mother, the Dawn Mother's priestess.

My mother didn't answer. She was standing upright in the boat, her face ashen.

One bird stood alone, on the roof of the shrine itself. The most beautiful of them all, white with a purity that made the rest of the world drab; graceful and majestic as a deity of the Sun Courts. It alone had a crest of dawn-bright feathers on its head, like a crown of flame. It looked straight at me with black, glittering eyes.

The Crane King, we call it. For surely it is the king, the leader of the demon-cranes who return each year. If we killed it, would the other birds retreat, like an army that has lost its leaders? Would the entire flock dissolve and fade, like ghosts at the sound of the Saadu priest's chant, like morning mist as it burns off in the sun?

No one can kill any of the birds. People tried, of course. They threw stones and shot arrows. They always missed. Each year, the cranes became more fearless — feeding even as boats glided within striking distance, lifting into the air before a pole could be swung, driving us back with the wind of their wings. And the fear grew. It was said that they could not be touched at all. It was said that to shed their blood was to be cursed. Worse: it was said that to shed their blood was to curse the lily crop itself.

But the crop was already cursed, from the first touch of those sharp pink beaks.

We still had a decent harvest, that first year. The lake is large, and back then the whole surface was covered with lilies. We couldn't drive the cranes away, but still there seemed enough for us all. They stayed a week, the most critical week of the harvest. The week when the nectar is at its most potent, able to cure deep-rooted prickle-fever, to bring cool rest and sleep to all ills: peace to sorrow, ease to pain. The week when the lilies glow brightest, their scent sweet with the Dawn Mother's breath. At that time, the nectar flows so rich and strong that you can actually see it glinting in the lily's heart; you can shake it into your pail.

Yes, we had a decent harvest, that first year with the birds. But even then we saw the taint they left behind — flowers turned white, drained of all essence. Ravaged lily patches which would never grow back.

Each year, those patches of ruined lilies grew.

And over the years, the complaints and suspicions from the merchants and city folk also grew. If we had demons attacking the crop, who was to say that demon-essence wouldn't enter the flowers, wouldn't seep into the lily wine or petals and stamens used for tea? Who could trust the medicine of the dawn-lilies?

The pilgrims who used to come for the blooming were spooked. Learned sages argued. Shamans and priests chanted and put on spectacular, useless shows at the lake's edge. Every year the cranes returned, beautiful and hungry.

Master Kevak holds the pouch of dried lily petals. I watch as he pours petals into his hand and sniffs them. He opens a jar of dried stamens. He holds to the light the single vial of lily wine we have left.

"How do you use these?" he says somberly, as though he doesn't know, as though he's never seen these medicines before.

I tell him. Tea from dried petals — the easiest and cheapest of the medicines. Good for simple pains, such as headaches and pulled muscles; good for nervousness, for inducing sleep and calm. Stamens for vigor, for a strong heart and kidneys. The lily wine ... I look at that last vial, and my voice dries as I think of what it could have cured, if only we'd had more.

We're sitting in the front room of my house, where my mother and I once treated patients together. The shelves are lined with jars of dried roots and powders and tinctures, some used in combination with lily medicines and some used on their own. Kevak wants to know about these combinations, too. He doesn't write anything down, the way I thought a scholar would. He seems to rely wholly on his memory.

"What is it?" I say, after he's asked me in exhausting detail for the recipe of a dried blackroot paste, used sometimes in conjunction with lily wine for childbirth fevers. "What are you trying to learn? How will it help?"

He shakes his head. "I don't know yet. Right now I just want to learn." He looks puzzled, his face intent. Sunlight from the open doorway glides across his finely cut features, catches and shines in his loose black hair.

My mother stirs in the next room, and I excuse myself to see her.

"Kai," she says, turning her head restlessly against the pillows. She'd been alert this morning, reasonably clear-minded; both wary and charmed by Kevak's courtesies, his respectful bearing and his proper gifts: candied fruit and sweet oranges from the nearby market town on the river; a bouquet of golden lilies; packets of fine white tea from the north.

I offer her lily petal-tea now. Her eyes hold mine, clear but troubled as she drinks. She grasps my wrist as I set the cup down.

"Be careful of that one," she says. She rolls her eyes to indicate Kevak in the next room.

"Why?" I whisper.

"He's too handsome."

I feel my face flush, but I don't suppress a smile. "Oh, Mother," I say. I roll my eyes, too. She should know that I'm not an innocent.

Later that same day I take Kevak back to the shrine. I show him the mesh racks we store there, used to dry lily petals and stamens. I show him the great copper kettles in which we boil the nectar down to thick syrup. Afterwards, he prays for a while before the Dawn Mother's altar, as he did on the first day we met.

While I wash and polish the carvings in the shrine, he takes my boat onto the lake. After a time, I come out onto the beach for a rest. I see him not far away, sitting cross-legged in the boat. He's reaching out to touch a lily. His fingers rest lightly against the pale bud, and he stays like that for a long moment, perfectly still. The closed flower glows against his fingers. What is he doing? He finally lets go, rises in one fluid movement and begins poling the boat away. I watch him growing smaller against the forest of lily buds. Every now and then I see him stop; he reaches out and touches another flower.

My mother taught both Suna and me about the lilies. She would take us to the lake when the dry season ended, and we would wade into the mud and plunge our hands underwater to reach for the first shoots, and then the first green leaves. We watched the buds form and grow. She taught us to look for the deepening color, a shift in the scent, a new softness in the leaves and closed petals. She taught us to take note of the rain and sun, to watch the movement of the sun beetles on the closed buds and the splash of the fish beneath the leaves. We learned to predict the precise moment of blooming, when the lilies open together as one.

But I've never been sure that I can feel the lilies' essence — not like Mother, not like my sister. I've held opened lilies in my hand at dawn; I've shaken the living nectar into my mouth. At the taste, I've felt sunlight coursing through my veins. But the essence? The sacred *ka*, the knowledge of the whole system of roots and shoots and leaves and flowers, spread throughout our sacred lake? The true grasp of what a dawn-lily *is*, its essential being, the essence that my sister claimed she could feel in the touch of petal or leaf?

And the Dawn Mother's voice: I've never heard it. I've sat up, sleepless and drunk on lily wine: our deity has never spoken to me. She's never given me a hint of what to do. I've never caught a glimpse of her or of the Heaven she came from, the golden Courts of the Sun.

Kevak helps me prepare the shrine. He's surprisingly easy to speak with, gently teasing when he's not absorbed in questions and herb craft. "No, you must let me show my respect," he chides softly when I protest to see him on his knees, scrubbing down the floorboards. He weaves palm garlands as skillfully as any old auntie. "I learned this as a boy, in my own family," he says when I look over his work approvingly. I had not thought it a common skill of city folk.

He has much to teach, too. He's brought his own medicines and shares them with me. "For dry-fever," he says, handing me a packet of red seeds. "For the water-sickness" — and he gives me a tin of salt crystals, speckled blue. Dissolved into liquid, the crystals will stop up a gut that's leaking waste and precious fluids; they'll save a life. I've never heard of such a thing before. "Where did this come from?" I ask.

He's spoken little of himself, but something lights in his face now. He tells me of a shining beach at the edge of a great ocean, near where the sun rises. He tells me of pools of seawater that collect on that beach and of how they dry out and leave the blue salt crystals behind. He hands me dried berries to treat the tremors of age, and he tells me of how they were harvested. The berries grow on thorny bushes on mountains so high that they nearly touch Heaven itself; the air there is so thin that only mortals born on the upper slopes can make the journey to the berry fields without fainting.

"You've been to these places," I say. It's not a question.

A flicker of surprise in his black eyes. As though to say, *She's caught me out.*

"Yes," he says. "I've been many places." He pauses. "I've always sought out knowledge. It's why I've come to your village now."

I've never been anywhere, not even to the city where my sister now lives.

"Are you from the capital?" I ask. "Is that where you were born?"

"No," he says. And now there's a sadness in the back of his eyes. The smile he gives me is rueful, but the longing in his voice is clear. "I came from elsewhere, like many students in the city. My home is in the east."

The heat of the sun wanes, and it's a bare week to the blooming. I announce the date, and the shrine is thronged with worshippers. All in the village now join in the preparations. Men stand on ladders to touch up paint on the shrine's roof, renewing shades of red and gold. Gold leaf is applied to the shrine's newly washed statues. Women bring in their own palm garlands and bright floral offerings. Incense burns, and there is at least one person to sweep out the shrine at the end of each day, making an offering of labor to our heavenly patron.

A few visitors and merchants from the nearby market town come to pray, but there are no pilgrims this year, no wealthy sightseers from the cities come to watch the lilies bloom. Kevak is the only one staying in the village lodging house.

Still, there's a new energy to the prayers and preparations this year. I feel it, too, even as I look out at the ruined lily patches. "A special blooming this year," my mother keeps saying. The convergence of the cycles for the Year of Fire and the Year of the Crane. Most had thought it an ominous sign. Wouldn't the Year of the Crane imbue the demon-cranes with more power? Wouldn't the Year of Fire inspire them with greater hunger for the dawn-lilies' flame? This is what the local Saadu priest in the market town preaches. Perhaps this is why we've had no city tourists this year.

But I wonder if the convergence means something else. Other people are wondering, too. I know that some of them have come to Kevak for medical help, most keeping it quiet from me and Mother for fear of giving offense. "He cured my headache," I hear a woman whisper as she looks toward Kevak. "That old ache in my knee is gone," I overhear an elderly man say. I watch the young doctor helping the men mix the great pots of paint outside the shrine. He's often here when not treating patients or poling a boat alone through the lilies.

A small crowd is gathered around him now. I watch as he greets an elder: he presses palms together and bows with perfect, formal grace. He turns his head to catch another greeting, and smiles. He draws the eye like the flight of a single bird against an empty sky.

"Kai." Someone is pressing a folded leaf of food into my hands. The village women always bring food to the shrine during these last days, both as offerings for the Dawn Mother and to feed the workers and worshippers. I take the leaf-packet of rice absently, and then recognize the giver as a woman who lost her son to the prickle-fever last year. My mother spent nearly the last of our lily-wine on him.

"Remember to eat," the woman says kindly. "Remember to take care of yourself."

Kevak doesn't ask me about the cranes. I've noticed that. I've had him to my home for meals; I've worked by his side. He's asked about every jar on my shelf of medicines; he's inquired after the rainfall this year, the history of our shrine, the amount of lily nectar harvested in a good year, and the recipe for the nut cakes he enjoyed at yesterday's breakfast. But he's asked me nothing about our demon-birds.

Doubtless others have told him. Doubtless he knows enough. But I find myself telling him anyway, as I sit in my boat and he poles us back to the main shore. We're the last to leave the shrine this day. The tiered roof glints behind us, new-painted. The sun is just beginning to set, and streaks of gold and orange light the sky.

The sky was like this when I first saw the cranes. Only the direction of the light was different. I tell Kevak this. I mention how beautiful the cranes were and are. I tell him of my first sight of them, speeding silently in from the east. I tell him that for those first few moments, I'd thought them a sign from the Dawn Mother herself. Her messengers. Her gift.

He's silent, watching me. That calm attention that draws words forth like the unspooling of a thread. I've seen it at work on others, on the few patients we've seen together.

"A sage from the mountains claimed that they're not demons at all," I say. "He said that they're *daino*, half-deities from the Courts of the Sun, and that they must be doing the Dawn Mother's bidding. He said it must be the gods' wish for the lilies to die." I don't add that the village barely gave the sage time to finish his pronouncement. Shouting with anger, the people had driven him away and into the wilderness, not even giving him a chance to retrieve his things from the lodging house.

"What does your mother say?" Kevak asks.

"The Dawn Priestess counsels patience." I hear the bitterness in my own voice. "For nearly seven years she's counseled patience, and faith in the Dawn Mother and all gods, and in continuing with our lives as best we can." I stop. My heart beats hard at my presumption, at the bitterness and doubt unveiled before another. This is no way for a Lady of the shrine to speak. But he's listening. I go on.

"My sister and her husband left the village three years ago. They went looking for work in the capital. We can't continue with our lives as before. There aren't enough lilies, and fewer people want to buy them anyway. The price keeps falling. Many people have left to look for work and homes elsewhere. They don't even come back for harvest anymore — there's no point." I don't mention Avan, the boy I thought I'd loved. He had left for the city, too, along with so many others.

"And you?" Kevak says. "What do you think the cranes are?"

I shake my head. "I don't know. Demons or deities?" I shrug. "When I was younger, I tried to shoot an arrow through the Crane King's heart."

Even in the failing light, I can see the shock on Kevak's face. I actually laugh a little.

"I didn't even fire the bow," I say. "I planned to. I'd hidden it in the shrine. Mother had told us all not to hurt the cranes; she said we would be cursed. And it seemed clear that you couldn't hurt them anyway. But I thought ..." I stop. I can't explain what I thought. I was young. I was angry. I thought that I could live with a curse, if it would save the lilies. Suna had followed her husband to the city that year, and Avan had left, too, the boy who'd claimed to love me.

Kevak is waiting. His stillness pulls at me. The shock has faded from his face, and he's just watching me, intent.

"I hid my bow in the shrine, under the altar cloth. I'd prayed to the Dawn Mother, and she said neither yes nor no. It was the third day of harvest, and I'd volunteered to stay on the island to tend the boiling nectar. So I was alone on the island when the cranes came."

I'm silent, remembering. I'd spent the previous days of that harvest memorizing the path of the birds' flight. I knew when the cranes would first appear. I knew when they would be visible from the open door of the shrine. I knew when the Crane King would come into range.

"I took my bow and arrow and waited in the shrine's doorway. I saw the cranes come. I don't think they saw me, waiting as I was in the dark doorway. But I could see *him*."

I would have seen him even if the dawn sky had been twice as dim. His crest of feathers glowed. His white breast shone like a moon.

"I nocked my arrow and lifted the bow, but ..." My voice stops. I could not loose the arrow. I could only stare, helpless, as the Crane King and his flock flew straight toward me, filling the patch of sky framed by the shrine's door. They were beautiful. Too beautiful. I let them fly past, disappearing from my sight over the roof of the shrine.

The sun fell as I told my story. There's only a hint of rose on the horizon now, fading into purple and blue.

Kevak seems to understand the words I don't say. "They cast a spell," he says softly. "They can't help it."

He'd paused in his poling, but now he begins to push the boat forward again. We're silent. There's only the shrill of crickets, the hum of insects rising around us. The occasional *plash* of a fish or call of a night-bird, lonely and echoing.

We land and drag the boat ashore. Kevak holds the lantern and walks me back to my house. We pause before I go in. "Even if you'd shot," he tells me, "you wouldn't have killed that bird. It doesn't work that way."

"Why not?" I demand. "What are they? What do you know of them?"

He shakes his head. "It doesn't matter, Kai." There's a bleakness in his eyes that startles me. And then his face shifts, and I see determination settle and harden his features. It's the determination I've sensed since first meeting him. "I will put an end to it," he tells me, like a promise. "An end to all of it."

That night I dream of the cranes again. I'm alone on the shrine island, in the silent dawn. This time I'm out in the open, standing next to the simmering kettle of nectar. The flock is distant, but nearing fast. I see the Crane King, his crest shining like the rising sun. I hold the bow in my hand, the arrow pulled back. The Crane King soars overhead, and I aim for his cloud-white breast.

And then Kevak is there, rushing past me. My hands falter in surprise. He cries something, in a language I can't understand, and the Crane King is plunging from the sky. Swifter than sight he dives and crashes into Kevak, and there's nothing but the whirl of feathers, the beating of wings, a white storm spinning on the ground. I can't see Kevak anymore, and I scream his name.

I wake up, my heart hammering.

Darkness. Darkness so total that I can't see a thing. In my mind, the birds' plumage still burns.

Gradually, I feel my heart slow. Familiar shapes resolve about me, and I hear Mother's breathing from across the room—shallow and fitful. As a child, I sometimes crawled into her bed for comfort from nightmares. Even a year ago, I would have woken her to hear her interpretation of my dream.

I don't wake her now. I lie in the dark, listening. I hear her turn restlessly; I hear her mumble to herself, half-words of no sense. She groans. And then she quiets again. Her breathing deepens, but it's still too irregular. I listen to those breaths, the uneven pattern of inhale and exhale, in and out, in and out, each breath like a tiny explosion in my own chest.

Just after the first light, I leave the house. I go to the village lodging house, raise my hand to Kevak's door. Before I can knock I hear a soft cough, and whirl to see Madhi, the woman who keeps the house and still cares for the few guests who come. She has a basket of steamed rice cakes slung on one shoulder; she's already on her way to make offerings at the shrine.

"Master Kevak left this morning," she tells me. "He told me to tell you that he would be back before the blooming."

I stand still, unable to phrase my rush of questions.

"He said he needed to gather some special herbs," Madhi says. Her eyes lock onto me with unabashed curiosity. "It's about the cranes, isn't it, Kai? The cranes and the blooming. Are you making a special potion with his herbs and the lily nectar?"

I start to shake my head and then stop. "Where—do you know where he's going?" I say faintly.

She shakes her head. "He left only moments ago. He was in a hurry—wouldn't stay for breakfast. Just took a couple nut cakes with him. I saw him headed down the road to town—maybe to take a boat from there?"

I thank her and hurry in that direction myself. I don't know what I'm thinking. I just want to speak with him.

I fairly run down the old cart track to the market town on the river, but I'm not far from our village when I see it. A glint of fire ahead of me on the road. The glow of dawn in the dust. And then a flash of white like lightning.

I slow, and as I come close I see that it's not a bit of glass or metal reflecting the sun, as I'd thought; it's not a dawn-lily opened and thrown on the ground as I'd thought even more briefly, crazily. It's a feather the length of my forearm. Pure white, except where it's tipped with the pink fire of dawn.

I kneel down to see it better. And then I notice the two leaf-wraps lying nearby. The kind of leaf-wraps that are used to hold sweet nut cakes.

❉ ❉ ❉ ❉

I wake my mother. I show her the feather. I need her to talk to me, to advise me. Surely she can do this. Surely she gathers strength as our lilies head toward bloom.

I tell her all about Kevak again, just in case she's forgotten who he is. I tell her about last night's dream. I let her touch the feather, and she runs trembling fingers up and down the spine.

"The *daino* are so vain," she sighs.

I stare at her.

"They could take any form they choose," she explains. "Old men, ugly men, crones with pock marks. But they always prefer to be young and beautiful. Too close to their natural forms. You would think that a half-god might hide better." She looks at me sharply, a reproving look I've known all my life. "You see," she says, "I did tell you that he was too handsome."

The next few days are a blur. I move through them like someone walking in her sleep. Most of the work of preparing the shrine is done and my continuous presence isn't required. I light incense at the altar in the morning, greet any worshippers, and return home to care for Mother. In the evening, I go back to help clean and dispose of the day's offerings. I gather the wilted flowers and food left in the shrine and give it all to the lake, our blessed lily lake formed by the palm print of the Dawn Mother. I watch the hungry fish rise for the crumbs.

"Ah, are you ready, Kai?" an old man asks me. "Are you ready?" says an older woman, giving me food to take back to Mother. Slowly it occurs to me that they're not just worried about the blooming and harvest rituals being overseen by an inexperienced young priestess. I look into the brown eyes of a woman I call "auntie," as I call all the older women of our village "aunt" and all the older men "uncle." They're worried about me, Kai. These women and men whom I've known all my life.

I'm ready, I tell everyone. I'll be ready.

Mother talks to me as though I'm a child again, telling me stories about the Dawn Mother and the Courts of the Sun. She asks me where Suna is. She doesn't remember Suna's husband when I mention him.

The night before the blooming, an auntie comes to stay with Mother so that I can spend the night alone in the shrine. I take the last precious vial of lily wine with me. Before the Dawn Mother's image, I kneel and tip the drops of wine into my mouth. The candle flames on the altar tremble and then steady again, casting shadow and light throughout the room.

I look upward at the central statue, into the Dawn Mother's jeweled eyes. She shines with new gold leaf. I empty my mind of everything save her face, open to whatever wisdom she might give me.

His step is soundless on the wood floor behind me, but somehow I sense it. Perhaps the lily wine or the Dawn Mother sharpens my senses. I turn to see him: a young man in plain dress, holding a cloth bag in one hand.

"Did you find them?" I say. My voice sounds strangely calm to myself. "Did you find the herbs you were seeking?"

"Yes." He steps forward. The candlelight washes across him. His beauty nearly makes me gasp. I realize that I'm seeing him with altered eyes: his true nature burns through his mortal dress like flame seen through a paper screen.

Now my voice does shake, just a little. "Was it far?" I say. "Far enough that you truly needed to fly?"

He moves swiftly, suddenly before me, kneeling across from me as I kneel. "Yes," he says again, and he opens his bag to show me a mess of thick black roots. "They needed to be harvested just before use. I learned about some of their properties from you."

"And what will you do with them?" I don't lift my eyes from the roots in his hands.

"Put a stop to it all. As I told you."

I look up, and he's the same and not the same: the angles of his cheeks and jaw, the curve of his lips. The dark eyes that meet mine with their familiar kindness. But there's something else in his eyes, too, something fierce and complex that I can't name. For the first time, I see the Crane King in him.

"Why?" My voice is dry, hardly above a whisper.

"Because I don't want to keep ravaging the Dawn Mother's fields, any more than you want me to. Listen, Kai." He doesn't touch me, but his eyes hold me fast. "For nearly seven years my people and I have been exiles, trapped in the form of cranes. For nearly seven years we've sought to overcome our curse and return home. We only take the dawn-lilies from need. They hold the strength of the sun, the blood of the dawn, the Dawn Mother's blessing; they're the essence of home for us. Do you see? Only these lilies have the *ka* we need to return.

"But there's another way. I thought of it, watching you and your people boil down the nectar in your great kettles. If I could concentrate the nectar's *ka*, bind it to the essence of other elements—earth-roots to bring us down from the sky, berries from the mountains nearest our home, salt crystals of the easternmost sea ... There could be a way to overcome the curse all at once. We wouldn't need to wait, slowly building our reserves with the harvest of each year. This year is special, the convergence of the Year of Fire and the Year of the Crane. It's for that reason that I can walk before you like this."

"Like this." A man who is a crane who is a *daino*. I feel laughter — incredulous, wild — welling up in me. I fight it down. "You're saying … this is the only year that it will work? This nectar mixture you mean to give your flock?"

"I'm the only one who need take it. Now, while in this form." His lips twitch in something like a smile, but there's too much of sadness in it. "They're tied to me, my people. They followed me from Heaven, and my form is theirs. I need break the spell only for myself, and they will be free as well."

I look away. I can't think while his eyes hold mine, and I know that I need to think. But he reaches out and catches my hands.

"Kai." His voice is low. "I need your help, as I said when I first came to you. Will you allow me the nectar harvest of the first three days? Will you ask your people to gather it? I can hold my own people off for that time. And then we'll never trouble you again."

I close my eyes. "My mother needs nectar, too. Concentrated and pure."

"She'll have it. A spoonful for her cure. But I need the rest."

More than a few spoonfuls of the concentrated nectar can kill a man. How much does this *daino* need? I keep my eyes closed. I'm walking a path I can't see, into a dangerous maze. Stories I've heard fill my mind: the battles and intrigues of the Sun Courts, the shifting alliances and betrayals of the gods and demigods, ruthless as those of human kings and even less knowable.

I open my eyes. "The Dawn Mother," I say. I'm not sure how to ask it. "Do you know her?" *Are you on her side? Is she on yours?*

"I do." His gaze now is soft. "Not well." He laughs a little, self-deprecatingly. "I'm not a king, or even a prince. I'm a very minor resident of the Outer Courts. But I've seen her. I honor her, Kai. She has no part in the quarrel that brought about my exile and curse."

You've only been killing her lilies for years. But she's never stopped him. What does she want? Year after year, the cranes of the Sun have come and taken what they pleased.

"Leave me," I mutter, and drop my gaze. "Let me speak alone with the Dawn Mother this night."

"Of course." He rises and bows, graceful as a palm tree in the wind. I watch his feet as they step away.

Words that he'd spoken days earlier echo in my mind. I'd told him of my first sighting of the enchanted cranes, and of how I was later unable to shoot their leader. He'd replied, *They cast a spell.*

I turn to the Dawn Mother and pray.

I was a child when Mother declared me her heir, years before the cranes ever came. I don't remember how she told me. I remember Suna crying about it. I remember Suna angry and red-eyed and running out alone into the night. And I remember that she came back silent and pretended to me that she was not angry or upset at all. "It is fine, Little Sister," she said, her chin lifted. And she never spoke of it to me again.

I didn't know what to think at that age. I knew even then that our goddess didn't speak to me as she did to Suna or my mother. I assumed that this would change as I grew older.

It was a few years later that I clapped at my sister's wedding. Happiness shone in her face like the sun, and happiness beat in my heart as well.

She would never have been able to marry as a priestess of the shrine. I looked upon her husband with fondness, as upon an older brother. I had no thought for marriage myself. I thought it good to be free of such ties. I knew that when I was old enough, I would discreetly take what lovers I pleased and bear children who carried my name and lineage rather than any man's. I would serve the Dawn Goddess as my mother taught me, and I would teach my children in turn.

And then the cranes came, and the lilies began failing, and our village and district became poor. Gold leaf in the shrine flaked and was not replaced. The paints on the temple grew dull. The younger people began moving to the cities for work. The boy whom I liked moved as well, and he married a girl in the city, a girl who could give him children with his name.

I followed my mother's bidding. I listened to all she said. My heart has not always been the perfect daughter's, but I tried my best. And then, last year, the illness swept in. The strong, wise priestess and mother I knew—stern and demanding but also compassionate and sure—slowly disappeared. The Dawn Mother doesn't speak to me, and I'm left alone in charge of the harvest.

❀ ❀ ❀ ❀

I wake with a start. My back is stiff from the wooden floor, and the candles have burned low. Through the shrine's open doorway I see lights on the lake; people are already on their way here, though there is yet no glimmer of dawn.

I step outside, and a shadow steps up beside me. Kevak. I don't look at him. I look at the nearest boat. I watch as it scrapes on shore. The two men aboard carry onto the island my mother, cradled in a hammock lined with pillows. It had been decided that she shouldn't miss this day, whatever her health might be.

I go to her, and in the lantern lights I see her face contorted in pain, her breaths too shallow. Her eyes pass over me without recognition or feeling.

"The first nectar is for her," I tell Kevak, who has walked to the boat with me. He nods, and gives me further instructions.

Then we turn to the gathering crowd and wait.

For the first time in seven years, the mysterious cranes of the east do not come. The skies are clear. I give the benediction and then, without lightness or laughter, with nothing but heart-speeding urgency, we begin the harvest.

We scatter across the lake, over the glowing water into a morning made vast with the birds' absence. Again and again I reach, the lilies just high enough that I have to strain a little from my sitting position, or else bend low from standing. I bend the blossoms gently and let the nectar run into my pail. In years past, we would have simply cut off the flower heads and roughly shaken the nectar out, throwing the drained blossoms into separate baskets for petal-tea and stamens. But there are too few good lilies now to use them thus, and we are not looking to harvest petals today. The living nectar is precious, and we need to come back to these same flowers over the next two days.

Kevak shares my boat with me, guiding us to specific lily patches that must have some potency I can't sense. His hands move tirelessly, yet I see that even he can coax no more than a small spoonful from each blossom. It will take more than ten times that amount to yield a single drop of visible, concentrated syrup.

All around me, others repeat my actions. Reach or bend, then tilt the lily head and shake it gently. Children and their grandparents, aunties and uncles, the few younger adults left. All working at this one task, all trying their best to gather enough nectar for the Crane King. Enough nectar to heal my mother, and enough to save us all.

We have the hours until the noon sun burns and the dawn-lilies begin to close.

"It's enough," Kevak says. He doesn't mean the nectar he needs for himself. He means the nectar syrup for my mother.

One of the shrine's large copper kettles simmers on the fire. Periodically Kevak adds a handful of crystals, a single red berry, torn black roots that look like fine hairs. The timing and amounts change according to some rhythm only he knows. But in a separate small pot pure nectar simmers, unmixed with anything else. This is the small vessel I tend and stir. All afternoon it's heated and now, as the sun begins to sink behind the hills, only a thick golden liquid, clear and irreducible, is left.

Carefully I transfer it to my vial. It's as Kevak said: exactly enough. He knew just how much raw nectar to spare for Mother's cure.

"Go," he tells me, smiling faintly. He stays with his kettle while I run to my boat and home, where Mother was borne back earlier in the day.

I rush into a house filled with people attending to the Dawn Mother's first priestess. Heads turn. "Kai," my mother says. Her face is tight with pain. I hold the vial to her lips and she drinks. And then she smiles. It spreads slowly on her drawn face: a clear, pure look of ease I've never seen on her before. Her eyes close. Her breathing becomes even and deep.

Kevak is at his kettle the next morning when I arrive. It occurs to me that he perhaps never left. There's only a hint of gray in the east.

"She's recovering," I tell him.

"Good," he replies.

I watch as he throws something into the kettle. Then his hands move rapidly, tracing signs in the kettle's steam, flowing scripts of air I cannot read. For a moment, the space between his hands glows like pale moonlight.

He drops his hands, and we stand in silence.

"When this is over," I say finally, "when you're done and gone — will the lilies recover?"

"They will."

"And you and your people will never return."

"Yes. It's part of our bargain, is it not?"

His voice is smooth and even. He stares down into the kettle's simmering depths, not looking at me.

"Yes," I say, and my chest feels tight. "It's part of our bargain."

I get back into my boat and return to the lily lake. I join the rest of my people, waiting for dawn with our pails.

He stays by his simmering potion all morning, no longer joining us on the lake. Every now and then I glance back, and I see him standing motionless by the kettle, straight as the tall bamboo.

In the afternoon, the villagers and I come back with fresh nectar. One by one, we empty our pails into the kettle. As the people come before Kevak, they each bow low and murmur their thanks. I can feel their awe. They think him a remarkable scholar, a talented shaman. I've told them all that he knows spells to keep the cranes away for three days. I've said that he'll guide us in preparing a special offering for the Crane King, a potion which will break a curse and send the cranes home. I haven't said who the Crane King actually is.

The last of the nectar is given; the villagers light incense and offer up prayers at the shrine. Kevak looks pale, still standing solemnly by the kettle. There are tables of food offerings that he is welcome to take — fruit, rice cakes, boiled eggs and fish and even meat — but I wonder if he's eaten anything at all.

"Thank you," he says, when I hand him a cup of water.

"Do you need anything else?" I ask.

He hands the drained cup back to me. "Not now." His eyes are glittering. "But tomorrow. When the final draught is ready. Could you be there for that?"

"Of course." I watch him uneasily. His eyes are distant, his voice and manner strained.

"Good." He looks at me directly then. Something in his face softens. His voice gentles; once again, he's the kind young man I knew. "But for now, you should go home to your mother."

❊ ❊ ❊ ❊

She's sleeping when I get there. The old auntie who's been watching her says that she was awake for part of the morning. "I told her everything," Auntie Sai says with pride. "How you've been leading the harvest. How you're working with Master Kevak. He's kept the cranes away two whole days already, and soon they'll be gone forever. It will really work this time, won't it?"

I think of all the times it didn't work, the visiting shamans and priests and monks of the past. "Yes," I tell Auntie Sai. "It will work."

I sit with my mother for a little while before supper. She's sleeping so peacefully. I watch the even rise and fall of her breast. I think of waking her. I think of telling her everything. I want to ask if what I'm doing is right, if the Dawn Mother approves. Or does she care at all? Has she noticed the blight of her flowers on earth, from where she sits in Heaven? I want to ask my mother about Kevak himself, of what she really thinks of him. But I don't do any of these things. I merely watch her breathing.

The third harvest morning. The last day that Kevak can hold his people off. If all goes well, they'll never come again.

All around me the lilies glow, brighter than the sky itself. Their rich scent fills my head. My hands are slippery with their soft petals. The clear nectar runs into the pail, and I reach for another flower, again and again.

Peals of children's laughter. I turn and see a boat glide past: a family, two little girls sitting between their parents, chattering in high, clear voices. I think that this time next year those girls will see a lake entirely covered with dawn-lilies, not a patch of open water to be seen. The Dawn Mother's glory will be restored. The lilies will flourish, and there will be lily wine and medicines to spare. Those little girls will know nothing different. No one will die of prickle-fever ever again.

The pink blossoms blur before me. I swallow hard.

That afternoon we give the last of the nectar to Kevak. He declares that it's enough. Relief sweeps us all, but there are no open cheers, no celebration yet. We need tomorrow to see if Kevak can fulfill his promise.

Again, the shrine fills with people. Incense sticks are lit, and the people prostrate themselves on the floor. The afternoon shadows lengthen as the people inside pray.

Kevak remains outside with the simmering potion. He stirs and throws in crystals like blue sparks of flame. His posture is still straight, but he looks paler than ever.

At last some of the villagers begin trickling back to their homes. I urge the rest on, saying that Master Kevak needs to prepare for tomorrow in peace.

"Come back tonight," he tells me, when only the two of us are left. "After the moon rises, meet me here." His eyes are the Crane King's again, glittering and strange. An energy seems to vibrate in him, an almost visible fire sparking about him. I promise, my heart beating hard.

Mother is awake when I come home. She's sitting up, her hair combed; her face is wan, but her eyes clear. Auntie Sai has made a simple supper of porridge and eggs and rice crackers for us—a convalescent's meal.

"Tell me," Mother says, after the auntie has left. Her gaze is as intense as Kevak's can be. "What is really happening, Kai?"

I tell her everything.

It comes out in a flood. I sit across from her over the supper dishes, and sometimes my words trip and stumble, but they keep on like running water. I tell her everything that's happened, from the moment that I first saw Kevak walking up the path to the Dawn Mother's shrine.

She closes her eyes and says nothing for a long moment. Then she shakes her head and sighs. "Ah, Daughter," she says. Her brow is creased with worry. "I don't know what we've stepped into here. This is larger than the Dawn Mother and her lilies. Far larger than us and our mortal cares. It's dangerous, mixing with *daino*."

"I know," I say. I feel sharp stones digging into my chest from within. I blink away the wetness in my eyes.

She sees, because she always sees. Her voice gentles. "You've done what you thought best."

"Are you saying it's not the right thing?" It comes out angrier than I meant.

"No. Sometimes we don't know what's right until long afterward. And you, Kai ... I know that you'll make your decisions for the right reasons. It's why I chose you over Suna."

"What?" The shift in conversation leaves me lost.

"Suna is smart and talented, yes," my mother says patiently. "Her heart is good. But that's not enough. I knew that you could make the hard decisions, for our people as well as our goddess."

"I …" I'm bewildered. "Aren't they the same thing?"

She smiles sadly. "Usually. Master Kevak is waiting for you now, isn't he? Go ahead; I'm fine here."

"But—" I'm not sure what I'm objecting to. "But—you know the Dawn Mother has never even spoken to me. Not the way she speaks to you."

"She will." Mother's voice is firm. "Go now, Kai."

So I do.

I don't see Kevak on the island when I arrive. The kettle fire is out. I panic only for an instant, before focusing on the light spilling from the shrine. From the brightness I see, every candle on the altar must be lit, and more.

He's inside, kneeling before the altar. All the statues of the Dawn Mother sparkle in the light. He holds himself so still, like a statue himself.

I come forward and kneel beside him.

"Kai." He doesn't turn his head. "I'm glad that you came." I see on the floor by his hand something I didn't notice before: a large golden cup set with red jewels. Liquid glints within.

"What would you have me do?" I ask quietly.

He doesn't look at me; he keeps his eyes lowered. There's a humble, beseeching quality to his voice I've never heard before. "Pray to the Dawn Mother on my behalf. Please. Ask for her favor for me."

I've done so for the past three days, but I bow my head now and pray again. I close my eyes and pray to my deity as intensely as I've ever done anything. I can feel my call to her, like something from within me flung out into the night, like a lantern beam reaching into the sky.

I don't know how long I kneel there. I open my eyes and find Kevak looking at me.

"Thank you," he says.

From a pocket in his shirt he hands me a small closed vial. A thick, golden liquid is contained within.

"I set aside some pure nectar syrup, apart from the main potion," he tells me. "If I look like I need it—if I seem to be in trouble—give me just a few drops. No more."

Before I can say anything, he turns and lifts the golden cup from the floor. In one motion, he tilts it and drinks it all down.

Nothing seems to happen. He sets the cup back on the floor, and his face is expressionless. He rises to his feet.

Then, even in the blaze of candlelight, I can see the color drain from his face. He sways.

I reach him just as he crumples to the ground.

He's breathing. Still breathing. I hold him in my arms. His breaths are fast and shallow, faster than my mother's ever were at the height of her illness, quicker than the breaths of any patient I've tended in illness or injury. His heart beats hard and fast as a bird's. His lashes flutter and I see his eyes jerk back and forth under closed lids.

I twist the cap off the vial he gave me. I hold the vial to his lips, tipping it so as to let the thick syrup slide down. *A few drops, no more.* Have I given too much already? Or not enough?

I kneel breathless beside him, watching and silently cursing him for not giving me better instructions, better warning.

Slowly, slowly, his breathing relaxes and deepens. Color comes back to his face.

"Kai." His eyes open and stare at me, calm as the waters of the lily lake.

I'm half-sobbing in fear and relief. "Why didn't you tell me? What happened? No, don't answer. Has it worked? Is the spell broken?"

"I don't know."

"You don't know?" My voice shakes. I realize that I'm trembling all over.

"Shhhhh." Still lying on his back, he lifts one hand and brushes away the tears on my cheek. His fingers are warm.

I catch his hand in mine. Our fingers interlace, and hold on.

"I'm sorry," he says. "The potion is … tricky. So many elements to balance. Hard to calibrate." He smiles faintly. "I'm not quite the herb master you might have thought."

"The pure nectar syrup," I say. "To balance out the potion's earth elements if they were too strong?"

He nods.

"But … but was the potion still enough to break the spell?"

Only now do I see something break his calm. Anguish, doubt, surfacing through those lovely eyes. "We'll know at dawn, Kai. That's why I wanted you here with me tonight. To be with me while I wait."

"And save your life if needed," I point out.

"That, too."

He tries to sit up, but I gesture him back down. I lie next to him. He reaches again for my hand.

"Tell me a story while we wait," he says. "Something from your childhood, before my people and I came for the lilies."

I have no stories, surely nothing of interest to a *daino* who has seen the gods of the Inner Courts of the Sun. But he asks after my sister, my friends, and I find myself telling him about catching frogs in the lake and fish in the flooded rice fields. I find myself talking about the harvest seasons of my childhood: the village thronged with visitors then; lame and ill pilgrims pulled by ox-cart through the streets and ferried to the shrine to pray; city tourists mincing through the village in rich silks; the shouting vendors hawking flowers and shrine offerings, snacks and sweets. My friend Avan and I would stuff ourselves on sweet, sticky breads brought from the capital, and then Mother would catch me and drag me to the shrine for my duties. I find myself talking about other holidays, the games

I used to play, the spotted brown cat I once kept as a pet. I talk about the uncle who used to take me hunting in the forest. The green light in the woods, the silence that became a song of bird calls and movement and wind if you listened. That uncle had made me my bow and arrow. He tried to teach Suna, too, but in this, at least, I was better than her.

My voice trails off. "Your turn," I tell Kevak. "Tell me about your home. Tell me about the Courts of the Sun."

He does. He doesn't speak of the events that led to his exile. Instead, he tells me about the view from his father's house: the great veranda that looks down over earth's mountains and fields, and up toward the white mountains of the moon. He tells me of the jade walls, the shining pavilions, the gardens of longan and lychee and fruits with no earthly equivalents. The blush of dawn on the city walls, the dawn-lilies that glow in every fountain and pond. The moonlight that falls at night like flakes of silver into the gardens, only to melt away with each day's light. The rush of wind when he and his brothers would leave their father's house, from time to time, to soar out over the earth in the borrowed forms of great cranes. The sound of thunder, and the dazzle of light when the gates of the Inner Courts opened, and he saw from afar the procession of the greater gods and goddesses.

He falls silent. We're lying together, the length of his side pressed warm against mine.

I turn to face him. This exiled divinity, who looks and feels so much like a beautiful young man. He stares back, and his hand lifts and tangles in my hair. He smells of nectar potion, of warmth and sweetness, spice and smoke. I lean in and press my face to his smooth, warm neck. His arm slips down to my back and pulls me in even closer.

And then I feel his body go rigid in my arms. A shudder runs all through him.

"What is it?" I whisper. But another shudder seizes him.

"Kevak!" I cry. I'm helpless, holding him and held by him, shaken by his tremors. Three, four, five. His eyes have gone glassy. It ends and I pull away, I'm on my knees, groping on the floor for the discarded vial of pure nectar syrup, thinking that I didn't give him enough, that this is some after-effect of the potion he took. But even as my hand finds and closes on the vial, Kevak himself is on his knees, panting.

"No," he says.

I stop and stare.

"No more," he gasps. "There's no chance at all if I take too much of that pure nectar, Kai."

I hold the vial tightly and crawl back toward him. He rests his head against my shoulder. I feel his heart beating. "It must be after midnight," he whispers. "My reprieve from bird-form was to last only this long—from my birthday to the anniversary of the curse."

The hours that pass now are like a terrible dream, delight and horror mixed. He holds me and I hold him; we lie curled together, now in silence and now with soft words. And then the shudders come, tearing at him, at regular intervals. Each time harder and longer. The battle of warring elements in his body: the spell that pulls him back to crane-form and the potion that strives to break it.

"I'm sorry," he tells me, during one of the moments of calm.

"No," I say, stroking his hair. "Don't be."

He's silent. After a long moment, not looking at me at all, he speaks again.

He speaks now of what happened when he left his father's house. He speaks of his years of exile, of wandering on the cold wind in a world drained of Heaven's light. Of looking into the flat, desolate bird-eyes of his followers, unable to speak and comfort them. Trapped in a form that had once been a joy and was now a curse. Hunger. Hunger that grew and grew; hunger for true sunlight, for Heaven's air, for the memory of Heaven's touch. Starving, he and his flock circled the world. Until they came to a lake of glowing lilies.

"They're the same as her lilies in Heaven," he says. "But even in Heaven there is no such lake, no place where they all grow together in such profusion … I saw your people on the lake. I remember seeing you." He looks at me now. "You were just a little girl, and I saw the shock and horror in your eyes. And later, I saw the hate."

I feel my heart go still.

His smile is a brittle, broken thing. His hand traces my cheek. "I didn't know," he says softly. "I knew, but I didn't. I didn't understand how much I'd hurt you and your people … Not until I came here in human form myself. It had been so long, Kai, since I talked to a girl. And you were grown up now, and beautiful, and I could see the *ka* in you; it's the Dawn Mother's light, it's kin to the strength of the lilies … And you made me welcome and served me tea and taught me what I needed to know. You offered friendship and aid even after knowing who I am, what I'd done. You're here with me now."

I feel the tears welling in my eyes again. I shake my head wordlessly.

"I'm sorry," he repeats. His eyes glimmer. "I'm so sorry."

I manage to swallow past the tightness in my throat. "I know," I say shakily.

"I mean that I'm sorry for what I may have to do."

There's a moment in which my mind spins, knowing that he's said something important but not understanding. "What?"

"I mean," and his words are slow now, deliberate, as he looks steadily at me, "that it all ends with this dawn. I am taking my people back home, no matter if the potion works or not."

"How—"

"They're my people, Kai. And there may be no other time. It's the Year of Fire and the Year of the Crane. This year we have the power to take all the lilies at once. We can go home."

"No." I draw back. "You can't."

"I can."

"But—"

"I'm sorry." His expression is terrible. There's shame in his face, pain and regret. But also an unbending determination, the cold, hard will of a lord of the *daino*.

"But why?" I feel the first trickling of rage. "Why do all this—the making of the potion, asking my people to harvest the nectar for you, all that we've done, all that you've done. This *night*!" I fling the word at him. What has it meant to him, to suffer and tremble and nearly die this night? To ask me here as witness to all that? "Why do all this when you've just meant to take the lilies, all of them, all along!"

"Because I don't want to take them all," he says simply. "It's as I said. I've always honored the Dawn Mother. I never wanted to destroy her lilies here. The lake in bloom is a marvel to rival anything in Heaven; the lilies are her miracle, born of her blood, her sacred, living touch upon the earth … I never wanted to desecrate them."

"Then don't." I'm crying openly now, unable to help it.

He reaches for me, and I jerk away.

Tears are spilling down his own face, glinting like sparks of fire. Is this how a *daino* cries? Is this for me? We watch each other across a space that's the bare length of an arm.

"Kai." Even now, in his pain and mine, he's beautiful. And it's all too much—this night, the endless revelations, everything. He moves toward me slowly, carefully, as though approaching a skittish animal, and I let him. I let myself collapse against him; I bury my face against his chest.

He holds me, and after a while the tremors take him again.

I count: twenty this time. Afterward, he lies on the floor limp and exhausted. His eyes are closed, and I think he's asleep. I think that the curse is winning, that he'll turn back to a bird soon. I think that all the gods and goddesses of Heaven can go to Hell.

He stirs.

"There's one more thing," he says. His voice is faint, a silver thread of itself. "You can come with me. Whatever happens, I can take you with when I leave."

He can barely move, but his eyes on me are clear and calm and utterly sure.

"You belong near the light of dawn," he says, "wherever that might be. And you would be honored in my father's house. I want you there,

Kai, by my side. I'll dress you in diamonds and emeralds, rubies and pearls. I'll show you the gardens, the fields of Heaven. And I'll show you all the places on earth that you long to see—the cities, the tops of those mountains where the sun-berries grow; the sea from which the sun rises each day … We'll be safe; there's nothing to fear. Once I've won us all back to Heaven, my father can keep us safe from my enemies."

His voice rises, gains strength as he speaks. But then I see him fading again under a tide of exhaustion. His eyes grow heavy-lidded.

"Kai," he whispers. "If you want … I'll make you my own. My Lady. If you can forgive me. I'll take you from here, away from mortal cares. We'll walk on the veranda under the river of stars …"

His eyes flutter. I watch them close.

I wait until he truly seems asleep. Then I pick up that vial of pure nectar syrup he gave me. I drink the last drops down.

Nothing happens at first. Kevak sleeps and the candles burn. I watch the light glinting off the altar statues. The candle flames are perfectly steady.

Gradually, I sense a silvery light. It's that faint lightening that occurs just before dawn, but it's not coming from outside. It's here, in the shrine, with me.

When she speaks, her voice is silvery, too: cool and quiet and calm.

"Daughter," she says, "it's not wise of you to love a *daino*."

"I know," I say. I'm drained, and my voice is empty.

She sighs like a whisper of wind. "He's clever, and his gesture is gallant. I do appreciate it, as he knew that I would. Of course, one might say that it's the least he could do, after desecrating my lilies for six years."

I shouldn't question my goddess. But it seems a shame not to try, when she's finally speaking to me. "Why did you let him do it?" I ask.

"Child, things are more complicated in Heaven than you can dream. I cannot always move openly." A pause. "And I was always fond of his father. The son plays a good game, gambling to keep my favor for his family. I did hope his plan would work."

"Are you saying it hasn't?"

"Not yet. But the dawn is not far off."

I think. "If he takes all the lilies today as he said, will that break the spell? And can you bring your lilies back?"

"Yes and no. I could only bring them into your world once."

There seems nothing to say after that. I wait, and the silvery light around me grows.

"Wake now," the Dawn Mother says. I open my mouth to ask one final question, but then I'm waking up on the shrine floor. The sky through the open doorway is white and gray with the light that comes just before dawn. I'm alone.

Alone. Kevak is gone.

Tears prick my eyes. And then the Dawn Mother gives me a parting gift of knowledge. Her instructions are laid out in my mind all at once, without words, clear as a drawn map.

I don't have to follow her instructions, I think. I never asked my final question, and so she never told me that Kevak didn't mean his last words. She never said that it wouldn't come to pass, that Kevak and I wouldn't be happy together in his father's house.

There is more than one goddess in Heaven, and plenty of gods. Am I bound to her alone, for the sake of my mother and my ancestors before? A pledge made generations ago, when the dawn-lilies first bloomed?

I watch the sky lighten through the shrine doorway. After a while, I get up. I step out into the morning light. And I go to the copper kettle.

No one is here today. The lake is utterly still. Kevak and I had warned all the villagers to stay away this morning, to allow the cranes' curse to be broken in peace. I wait, and the sun's first rays shoot past the horizon. The lilies begin to unfurl.

The cranes appear as lines in the sky, dark against the sun.

They come on as swiftly as ever, and soon I see Crane King in the lead, his crest of feathers glowing.

I think that surely he must see me. He must know what I mean to do. I'm not hiding within the shrine this time, and he must know that this time I'll do it.

I nock the arrow and lift my bow. The bow and arrow that I've kept hidden in the shrine, as I've done each year since the first time I tried this. He's right that I could have never hurt him before. No ordinary arrow would wound him. But this arrow was dipped into the remains of his nectar potion, into the last few drops clinging to the bottom of the kettle. Just a few drops are enough, plunged into his heart.

I need break the spell only for myself, and they will be free as well.

Is this why Kevak keeps flying straight toward me? Does he know, as the Dawn Mother has given me to know, that this is yet another way to set his people free?

He's nearly within range. I pull back on the bow-string as my uncle taught me. My uncle who was really my father, although it wasn't something we could speak openly of. He was one of the first to die last year, when our supply of lily wine ran so low.

The Crane King is nearly above me. Abruptly, the rest of the flock veers to the side. But Kevak keeps straight toward me, and I swear that his flight has somehow slowed.

With a prayer, I loose the arrow. I see it hit home. In the moment before he falls, I see the blood spread over his cloud-white breast: a stain of brilliant pink the color of lilies, the color of dawn.

About the Author

Vanessa Fogg dreams of dragons, selkies, and other oddities from her home in western Michigan. Her short stories have appeared in number of science fiction and fantasy magazines, as well as in a few non-genre venues. For more, visit her website at vanessafogg.com.

About the Publisher

Annorlunda Books is a small press that publishes books to inform, entertain, and make you think. We publish short books (novella length or shorter) and collections of short writing, fiction and non-fiction.

Find more information about us and our books online: annorlundaenterprises.com/books or on Twitter: @AnnorlundaInc.

To stay up to date on all of our releases, subscribe to our mailing list at:

annorlundaenterprises.com/mailing-list

Other Titles from Annorlunda Books

Short eBooks

Unspotted, by Justin Fox, is the story of the Cape Mountain Leopard and the author's own journey to try to see one.

Okay, So Look, by Micah Edwards, is a humorous, yet accurate and thought-provoking, retelling of the Book of Genesis.

Navigating the Path to Industry, by M.R. Nelson, is a hiring manager's advice on how to run a successful non-academic job search.

Don't Call It Bollywood, by Margaret E. Redlich, is an introduction to the world of Hindi film.

Collections

Missed Chances is a Taster Flight collection of classic stories about love, all with a hint of "the one that got away."

Love and Other Happy Endings is another Taster Flight of classic stories, all of which end on a high note.

Academaze, by Sydney Phlox, is a collection of essays and cartoons about life in academia.